Overc

Sports Biographies

Home Run Heroes

by

John Bergez

Don Johnston Incorporated
Volo, Illinois

Edited by:

Jerry Stemach, MS, CCC-SLP
Speech/Language Pathologist, Director of Content Development, Start-to-Finish® Books

Gail Portnuff Venable, MS, CCC-SLP
Speech/Language Pathologist, San Francisco, California

Dorothy Tyack, MA
Learning Disabilities Specialist, San Francisco, California

Consultant:

Ted S. Hasselbring, PhD
William T. Brian Professor of Special Education Technology, University of Kentucky

Graphics and Illustrations:

Photographs and illustrations are all created professionally and modified to provide the best possible support for the intended reader.

Narration:

Professional actors and actresses read the text to build excitement and to model research-based elements of fluency: intonation, stress, prosody, phrase groupings and rate. The rate has been set to maximize comprehension for the reader.

Published by:

Don Johnston Incorporated
26799 West Commerce Drive
Volo, IL 60073

800.999.4660 USA Canada
800.889.5242 Technical Support
www.donjohnston.com

DON JOHNSTON

International Standard Book Number
ISBN 1-893376-43-5

Contents

Chapter 1

The Hardest Thing in Sports

UPI/CORBIS-Bettmann

Babe Ruth (1895-1948).

Hitting a home run is the most exciting play in baseball. It is also the hardest thing to do in sports.

Why is it so hard to hit home runs? Imagine that you are standing in the batter's box. The pitcher throws, and a spinning white ball speeds toward you at 90 miles per hour. In less than one second, it might smash into you. Your body wants to jump out of the way. Fear is a hitter's worst enemy.

Somehow you have to stay loose and concentrate on the pitch. How fast is it going?

Will it stay straight, or will it curve or drop? You have one-tenth of a second to make up your mind and start your swing. After that it's too late.

You need to be as quick as lightning and very strong to hit a home run. You have to meet the ball at exactly the right instant. And you have to meet the ball at just the right spot on the bat. If you miss that spot by one-eighth of an inch, the ball will pop up, and you will be out.

It takes a special player to do all of this well. And it takes a very special player to set a home run record.

This book is about five very special players. They have set the greatest home run records in the history of major league baseball.

The story starts with Babe Ruth. Ruth was the first home run hero. He was one of the best baseball players who ever lived, and baseball fans loved him.

In 1927, Babe Ruth set the first great home run record.

UPI/CORBIS-Bettmann

Roger Maris swings and hits his 61st homer of the 1961 season.

He hit 60 home runs that season. In 1961, Roger Maris beat Ruth's record by hitting 61 homers. But Maris's season was eight games longer than Ruth's season, so some people said that the new record shouldn't count. They still loved Babe Ruth and they hated to see him get knocked out of the record books. Breaking Ruth's record was hard for Maris. It was even harder for Maris to see that so many people were against him.

Babe Ruth also set another great home run record. He hit 714 homers in the major leagues. No one came close to this record for almost 40 years. Then Hank Aaron broke it in 1974. Once again some baseball fans were angry that someone was breaking one of Babe Ruth's records. Some white fans even insulted Aaron and threatened him because he was a black man. But Aaron stood up to them. He became one of baseball's greatest heroes.

He is still the all-time home run champion because he hit 755 home runs during his baseball career.

In 1998, Mark McGwire and Sammy Sosa put on the most thrilling home run race ever. By late summer, both of them had the chance to break Roger Maris's record for the most home runs in a single season. There was a lot of pressure on Big Mac and Slamming Sammy, but they kept on blasting home runs anyway. When the season was over, both men had broken the record.

Agence France Presse/CORBIS-Bettmann

In 1998, Sammy Sosa was in a home run race with Mark McGwire.

All five of these men had to overcome some bad times. All five of them were brave, talented, and hardworking. They are baseball's greatest home run heroes.

Chapter 2

Babe Ruth: The Kid from Baltimore

CORBIS-Bettmann

Babe played for the Boston Red Sox from 1915 until 1920.

Babe Ruth was born in 1895. His real name was George Herman Ruth. When George was a young boy, he was always getting into trouble. He hung out on the streets of Baltimore with other rough kids. He liked to throw apples and eggs at truck drivers. He got into fights. He stole things and ran away from the police. Sometimes his father beat him for skipping school. After Ruth grew up, he said, "I was a bum when I was a kid."

When George was 8 years old, his parents gave up trying to control him.

They took him to St. Mary's School for Boys, and they left him there.

St. Mary's was a little bit like a jail. The boys lived at the school even during the summer. George was sad that he hardly ever saw his family. "I guess I'm just too big and ugly for anyone to come see me," he told his friends. "But maybe next Sunday someone will come to see me."

George grew up at St. Mary's. He became a tall, strong teenager with broad shoulders and big muscles. He was the school's star baseball player.

He could run and hit, and he was great in the field. He was also a powerful pitcher.

George's skill at baseball gave him a way to get out of St. Mary's. In the spring of 1914, a minor league team offered him a job, so George left St. Mary's at last. He was 19 years old. His favorite teacher wished him luck. "You'll make it, George," the teacher said.

That summer the Boston Red Sox hired George as a left-handed pitcher.

CORBIS/Bettmann-UPI

In 1914, Babe Ruth was a pitcher for the Boston Red Sox.

By that time some of his teammates were calling him "Babe." The nickname fit him. He was like a little boy in a big man's body. After the strict rules of St. Mary's, he loved being able to do whatever he wanted. He was thrilled by his first train ride and by trips to big cities. He rode hotel elevators up and down just for the fun of it. He gobbled six hot dogs at a time and washed them down with six sodas.

He spent his money as fast as he earned it. He was loud and crude and he was full of life.

He was also the best left-handed pitcher in baseball. Between 1914 and 1919, he won 89 games and lost only 46.

Babe Ruth even set a record for pitching in a World Series. At the end of every season, the best team from the American League plays against the best team from the National League to see which team will be the World Champions.

CORBIS-Bettmann

Babe Ruth could hit the ball higher and farther than anyone had ever seen.

The team that wins more games wins the World Series. Babe Ruth pitched almost 30 innings in a row in World Series games without the other team scoring a single run. He was on his way to winning a place in the Hall of Fame.

But Babe loved hitting even more, and he hit like no one else did. In those days, baseballs were softer than they are today, so they didn't go as far when a batter hit them. Home runs were rare. Most hitters just tried to punch the ball past the infielders.

But Babe was different. He swung so hard that sometimes he nearly fell down. And he could hit the ball higher and farther than anyone had ever seen.

By 1919, Babe was playing in the outfield so that he could hit more often. An outfielder can play every day, but a pitcher must skip a few games to rest his arm. That year Babe amazed baseball fans by slugging 29 home runs. It was a new major league record.

Nobody else in the American League hit more than 10 that season.

That was the first season that Babe played every day. Baseball would never be the same again.

Chapter 3

The Home Run King

UPI/CORBIS-Bettmann

In 1923, Babe Ruth began to play for the New York Yankees.

Before Babe Ruth, baseball was a game of hits and bunts and stolen bases. Teams tried to score one run at a time. Nobody thought much about home runs.

Babe's slugging changed all that. Baseball fans loved to see his booming hits. They loved the way that a home run could suddenly turn a game around. They were catching home run fever.

Soon the team owners began changing the rules to help the batter.

They changed the way that baseballs were made so that a ball would go farther when the batter hit it. Almost overnight, baseball changed into a hitter's game. And it was all because of Babe Ruth.

Meanwhile, Babe's life was changing, too. In 1920, the owner of the Red Sox needed money badly. He got the money by selling Babe and some other star players to the New York Yankees.

The Yankee fans were thrilled. They filled the ballpark to watch the great young slugger. That year, Babe stunned everyone by hitting 54 home runs. He hit more home runs by himself than all of the players on any other team together! But in 1921, Babe was even better. He blasted 59 home runs. He set a new home run record for the third straight year.

Babe was on top of the world. People called him "The Babe" and "The Home Run King." He was the biggest name in baseball.

In fact, everything about him was big. Babe himself said, “I swing big, with everything I’ve got. I hit big or I miss big. I like to live as big as I can.”

Babe was living big all right. One of his teammates said that Babe was like a hungry kid with a truckload of candy. He was always looking for fun and excitement. Often he stayed out all night. One time a reporter asked Babe’s roommate, “What is it like to room with the Babe?” The roommate answered, “I wouldn’t know. I only room with his suitcase.”

UPI/CORBIS-Bettmann

Babe Ruth said, "I swing big, with everything I've got. I hit big or I miss big."

In 1922, Babe's lifestyle began to catch up with him. He gained too much weight. He fought with his manager and the umpires. He was suspended five times, so he missed some of the games that he was supposed to play in. He hit only 35 homers and lost the home run title. Yankee fans felt that Babe had let them down. They booed Babe until his ears burned.

That winter, Babe was a guest at a dinner for sports writers. After the dinner, a New York state senator gave a speech.

He said that Babe was letting everybody down, especially the little kids who admired him.

When Babe got up to speak, he had tears in his eyes. He said that he was going to go home and work hard to get back into shape. He promised to behave himself. He said that he wouldn't ever let anyone down again.

Babe kept his promise for two seasons. He led the league in home runs in 1923 and again in 1924.

Then he went back to his old ways. In 1925 he became sick and missed a lot of games. He was suspended for fighting with his manager. The Yankees fell to seventh place.

That was Babe's worst season. He was only 30 years old, but he seemed fat and worn out. Most people thought that his days as a great player were over.

Chapter 4

Two Magic Numbers

CORBIS/Bettmann-UPI

In 1932, Lou Gehrig greets Babe Ruth at home plate after Ruth hit a home run in the World Series against the Cubs.

Babe was determined to bounce back after his terrible season in 1925. He worked out very hard that winter. The next year he led the league with 47 home runs. Babe was back on top, and so were the Yankees. But the best was still to come.

In 1927, the Yankees stayed in first place all season. The big story was the home run race between Babe and his teammate Lou Gehrig. First, one of them would pull ahead, and then the other one. On September 7, the two friends were tied with 44 homers.

Then Lou started to cool down, and Babe shot ahead.

Babe stayed hot all month. Suddenly, he was getting close to his own record of 59 home runs in one season. All over the country, people began asking the same question: "Did Babe hit one today?"

On September 29, Babe homered twice. Now he had 59. He needed one more to break the record. There were two games left.

UPI/CORBIS-Bettmann

Babe Ruth hits his 60th home run of the 1927 season.

The next day Babe came up to bat in the eighth inning against Tom Zachary of the Washington Senators. On the third pitch, Babe swung hard. Whack! The ball took off straight toward the seats in right field. Yankee Stadium shook with the roaring of the fans. Even the reporters in the press box stood up and cheered. Babe Ruth had outdone himself again. He had hit his 60th home run.

Babe couldn't believe it himself. After the game, he said, "I never thought I could do it. Let's see some other monkey hit 60!"

Babe led the league in homers again the next year, and for three more years after that. He had a big belly, and he looked funny running around the bases. But he could still whip that bat around!

In 1932, Babe hit his most famous home run. It came in the World Series against the Chicago Cubs. Babe had already homered once that day.

When he came up to bat in the fifth inning, the Cubs and their fans were screaming at him and calling him names because they knew that he could win a game with one swing of the bat.

But Babe stayed cool. He let two strikes go by. Then he seemed to wave his hand toward the bleachers in center field. On the next pitch, he swung. The ball soared high and far over the fence in center field. Babe laughed all the way around the bases. "You lucky son of a gun," he said to himself.

Did Babe really mean to promise a home run? Nobody knows for sure. But if anybody could do it, Babe could.

In 1935, Babe left the Yankees and joined the Boston Braves. He could barely play anymore. He was fat and slow and clumsy. But the old slugger had one great moment left. On May 25, he hit three home runs in the same game. The last one sailed clear over the roof of the stadium. It was his 714th home run in the major leagues.

A week later, Babe quit baseball for good. He held many records, but two of them stood out. They were the two magic numbers of 60 and 714. From now on, every home run hitter knew about those numbers and every home run hitter would be chasing the Babe.

Most people thought that no one would ever catch him. And for many years, no one did.

Chapter 5

The M and M Boys

UPI/CORBIS-Bettmann

Roger Maris reads about Babe Ruth at Yankee Stadium in 1961.

In 1960, the New York Yankees were the kings of baseball. They had won eight pennants in ten years. They were a team of great stars. The greatest star of all was Mickey Mantle. Mickey had already won three home run titles. Some of his booming homers reminded people of Babe Ruth.

The Yankees also had a new player that year. His name was Roger Maris.

Roger Maris wasn't a famous star at that time but he was a very good all-around player. He was fast on the bases and he was a fine fielder.

He also had a strong throwing arm. He could hit, too, but not like Mickey Mantle or Babe Ruth. Still, the Yankees thought that his left-handed power was just right for Yankee Stadium.

That first year, Roger surprised even the Yankees. All season he battled Mickey for the home run championship. Mickey won, 40 to 39. But Roger led the league with 112 runs batted in. He also won a Gold Glove for his fielding skill. He was named the American League's Most Valuable Player.

Roger was proud of his great year. But he was a little scared by it, too. What if he never had such a good season again?

The next year, Roger started out badly. He worried about his low batting average, and he wasn't hitting home runs. The Yankees told Roger to relax. Don't worry about hitting for a high average, they told him. We just want you to hit homers and bat in runs.

After that, Roger took off. He smashed 24 homers in the next 30 games.

Even Babe Ruth never had a streak like that! Mickey was hitting, also. By early July, Roger had 34 home runs and Mickey had 33. Now everybody was talking about Maris and Mantle. Newspapers started calling them the M and M boys.

Baseball fans were getting very excited. The M and M boys were in a great home run race. Even better, they both had a chance to break Babe Ruth's magic record of 60 home runs in one season.

UPI/CORBIS-Bettmann

The M and M boys in July 1961: Mickey Mantle and Roger Maris play side-by-side as New York Yankees.

There was only one problem. In 1961 the American League began playing 162 games. The old season was only 154 games. What if it took more than 154 games to break Babe's record? Should the new record count?

At that time, a man named Ford Frick was in charge of baseball. Frick was once a good friend of Babe Ruth's. In July, he made a ruling. He said that a player had to hit 61 homers in 154 games or less. Otherwise, Babe's record would stay.

The new one would have a special mark in the record books to show that the record was set in more games.

Frick's ruling seemed to change the rules in the middle of the season. The M and M boys knew that they weren't just chasing each other anymore. Now they had to chase the ghost of Babe Ruth, too.

Chapter 6

A Record of His Own

UPI/CORBIS-Bettmann

Roger Maris (1934-1985).

At first, Roger Maris didn't worry about Ford Frick's ruling. He didn't think he could hit 60 home runs anyway. But by early September, Roger had 53 homers. Mickey was right behind him with 51. The whole country was watching the race for Babe Ruth's record.

Then Mickey's leg became infected, and he couldn't play. "I'm finished," Mickey said. "I can't do it. I hope Roger can."

But for Roger, the race was turning into a nightmare. Roger was a shy and private man. He hated the way that strangers and reporters crowded around him now. He felt as if people were watching every little thing he did. He began to feel like a monkey in a zoo.

Worst of all, many fans were making it hard for Roger. Some of them booed whenever he didn't hit a home run. Others said that he wasn't good enough to challenge Babe Ruth.

UPI/CORBIS-Bettmann

Roger Maris swings and hits his 61st home run.

They didn't want Roger to break the Babe's magic record of 60 home runs.

Roger didn't understand why people were attacking him. "I know I'm not Babe Ruth," he said. "I'm just Roger Maris."

As the pressure kept building, Roger felt like he was getting sick. His face broke out in a rash. Clumps of his hair began falling out. For the first time in his life, he hated going to the ballpark. "I can't stand it anymore," he told his friend, Mickey.

"You have to stand it," Mickey answered.

By game 154, Roger had 58 homers. He needed three more to break the record.

Before the game, Roger was shaking all over. He had to force himself to go out and play. That night he got his 59th home run. But it was the best that he could do.

Roger was exhausted. He wanted the season to be over. Still, he knew he had a chance to set his own record for 162 games. He made up his mind to try.

By the last day of the season, Roger had 60 homers. He needed one more to become the first player to hit 61 home runs in one season.

In the fourth inning, Roger came up to bat against Tracy Stallard of the Boston Red Sox. Stallard's third pitch was a fast ball. Roger's eyes lit up. As soon as he hit the ball, he knew it was gone. He had hit number 61!

Mickey Mantle was watching the game on television in his hospital room.

UPI/CORBIS-Bettmann

In this photo, Roger Maris has just hit his 61st home run on October 1, 1961.

He whooped and clapped when he saw the ball go into the right field seats. Mickey knew how hard it was for his friend to set the record. Later Mickey said that it was the greatest performance in the history of sports.

Back at Yankee Stadium, Roger was in a daze. He kept his eyes to the ground as he ran quickly around the bases. He barely heard the roaring crowd.

But for once, the Yankee fans wouldn't stop cheering for Roger Maris.

Again and again, his teammates pushed him out of the dugout so that he could wave to the crowd.

At that moment, Roger was doing something that he hadn't done in a long time.

He was grinning from ear to ear.

Chapter 7

"Hammering Hank"

UPI/CORBIS-Bettmann

Hank Aaron of the Milwaukee Braves in 1954.

Henry Aaron was born in 1934. When he was a little boy, he told his dad about a special dream.

Mr. Aaron said, “Tell me about your dream, Hank.” Everyone called Henry by his nickname, Hank.

Hank looked at his dad and said, “When I grow up, I’m going to be a baseball player!”

Mr. Aaron just nodded and smiled. He knew that black players weren’t allowed in the major leagues. The white players and the team owners had made that decision back in 1887.

Mr. Aaron shook his head. It was the 1940's now, and people in America still didn't treat black people fairly.

Mr. Aaron didn't want to spoil his son's dream. He knew that Hank would find out soon enough.

Hank's family lived in Mobile, Alabama. They lived in a poor part of town. The street where they lived was made out of dirt. Mr. Aaron had built their house out of used wood. He got the wood for their house from another house that was being torn down.

Their bathroom was a shed out in the back yard. The Aarons were poor, but they were proud that they owned their own home.

Hank played baseball every chance that he got. He didn't have money to buy real baseballs and bats, so he practiced hitting bottle caps with a stick. Sometimes he made baseballs by wrapping old stockings around golf balls.

When Hank was 12 years old, something amazing happened. It was 1946 and the Brooklyn Dodgers hired a black player named Jackie Robinson. He was the first black person to play baseball in the major leagues in more than 50 years! Black Americans were thrilled. They knew that black players were just as good as white players. Now they had a chance to prove it!

Jackie Robinson became Hank Aaron's hero. Hank was small and skinny, but he still had his dream.

CORBIS/Bettmann-UPI

Hank Aaron played as an outfielder for the Milwaukee Braves.

He told his father, “I’m going to be in the big leagues before Jackie quits playing.”

But getting to the major leagues wasn’t easy. First Hank had to prove himself in the minor leagues. When he was 19, he became one of the first black players in the Southern League. Many white people in the South weren’t ready to see black men and white men playing baseball together. Some white people threatened to shoot any black players who dared to play.

But Hank was so good that he began to change people's minds. He won the Southern League's Most Valuable Player award. By then, even the white fans were cheering for him!

At last, Hank made it into the big leagues. By 1954, Hank was playing for the Milwaukee Braves. That spring, Mr. Aaron saw his son play against Jackie Robinson and the Dodgers!

In Milwaukee, Hank became one of the best hitters in baseball. Pitchers were afraid of him. He smashed line drives all over the field.

Players admired his quick wrists. One pitcher complained, “Trying to sneak a fast ball past Hank Aaron is like trying to sneak the sunrise past a rooster.” Hank’s fans called him “The Hammer” and “Hammering Hank.”

Hank’s favorite year in Milwaukee was 1957. That season, he hit a home run to win the pennant for the Braves. Hank’s teammates lifted him up and carried him off the field. It was Hank’s happiest day in baseball.

But Hank wasn't happy for long. The next morning, the newspaper showed a mob of white people screaming at black students in Little Rock, Arkansas. The mob didn't want black children in their schools. Hank wondered, "When will everyone in America learn to respect my people?"

Chapter 8

Chasing the Dream

UPI/CORBIS-Bettmann

Hank Aaron shows the ball that he hit to break Babe Ruth's home run record.

In 1966, the Braves moved to Atlanta, Georgia. Hank Aaron was the Braves' best player. He was an All-Star every year. But only a few people seemed to know how good he really was.

Hank wanted more people to know how well he could play baseball. He knew that he could hit more home runs in Atlanta. That's because the ball travels farther in warm, light air. So Hank decided to try for more homers.

Year after year, Hank got more and more home runs. Suddenly, people realized that Hank was getting close to Babe Ruth's record of 714 home runs. Some fans didn't want anyone to break Babe's record. And some people didn't want a black man to break the record.

Hank started getting ugly letters and phone calls. Some of the letters started, "Dear Black Boy." Most of them were worse than that. One letter said, "If you hit one more home run, it will be your last."

Hank's parents got phone calls, too. Some of the callers said that they would kill Hank.

The insults and threats only made Hank try harder. "I had to break that record," he said later. "I had to do it for Jackie, and my people, and myself. And for everyone who ever called me a bad name."

Hank talked about the letters and phone calls. Soon thousands of other people began writing to him. They told Hank that they were cheering for him.

CORBIS/Bettmann-UPI

Hank Aaron ties Babe Ruth's home run record during the first game of the 1974 season.

Hank especially liked the letters from children. "They're the best fans in the world," he said.

When the 1974 season started, Hank had 713 home runs. He needed just one more to tie the record.

Hank didn't waste any time. In his very first game in Cincinnati, Ohio, he hit his 714th home run. He had tied Babe Ruth!

Three days later, the Braves played the Dodgers in Atlanta. The stands were filled with 53,000 excited fans.

Millions of other fans were watching on television.

The first time that Hank came up to bat, the pitcher walked him. The crowd groaned.

Hank's next chance came in the fourth inning. He told a teammate, "I'm gonna get it over with right now." He did it, too! He blasted the second pitch over the fence in left field. On the radio, the Braves' announcer yelled, "There's a new home run champion of all time, and it's Henry Aaron!"

UPI/CORBIS-Bettmann

Hank Aaron hits his 715th home run on April 4th, 1974.

When Hank crossed home plate, his father was there to greet him. Then his mother came running up. She threw her arms around Hank and wouldn't let go. Hank said later, "I never knew she could hug so tight."

That night, Hank got down on his knees to pray. Tears ran down his face as he thanked God for helping him through his hard times.

Hank Aaron quit baseball in 1976. He had 755 home runs and 2,297 runs batted in. Those are still the all-time records.

In 1999, the sport of baseball honored Hank by creating the Henry Aaron Award. The award is given to the best hitter in the major leagues each year. The CNN company honored Hank, too. It gave him one million dollars for his favorite project. Hank's project helps poor children who want to learn about music, writing, art, dance, and sports.

Hank calls his special project "Chasing the Dream."

Chapter 9

Big Mac and Slamming Sammy

CORBIS/AFP

Sammy Sosa and Mark McGwire.

It seemed as if all of America went baseball-crazy in 1998. That summer, Mark McGwire and Sammy Sosa put on the greatest home run race in history. The best part was that everyone seemed to like them both. People called Mark McGwire "Big Mac," and they called Sammy Sosa "Slamming Sammy."

The two sluggers looked very different. Big Mac stood almost six-and-a-half feet tall. His thick arms looked like tree trunks.

Sammy was six feet tall and very strong, but he looked tiny next to Mac.

Mac and Sammy came from very different places, too. Mac grew up in southern California. His father was a dentist, and his family had a comfortable life. As a boy, Mac played baseball in Little League.

Sammy came from a poor country called the Dominican Republic. It is near Cuba and Jamaica. Sammy's father died when Sammy was 7 years old. Young Sammy had to earn money to keep his family from starving.

CORBIS/AFP

Sammy Sosa worked hard at becoming a better hitter.

He sold oranges for a dime each and polished a pair of shoes for a quarter. He didn't start playing baseball until he was 14. He had to use an old milk carton for a glove.

A baseball scout brought Sammy to the United States when Sammy was 17. Sammy had a lot of talent, but nobody had ever really taught him how to play baseball. He swung at bad pitches. He made wild throws. People began calling him "Sammy So-So." Sometimes he wanted to give up and go home.

Then the Chicago Cubs took a chance on Sammy. The Cubs told Sammy that they believed in him. He worked hard at becoming a smarter hitter. Sammy felt like an important part of the team, and he started enjoying himself more.

Unlike Sammy, Mac started out as a star baseball player. But then he began to struggle. In 1991 he batted only .201 and hit just 22 homers. Kids near his house yelled, "Mac, you stink!" Then he started getting hurt and missing a lot of games.

Agence France Presse/CORBIS-Bettmann

Mark McGwire hits another home run.

Mac's life was unhappy in other ways, too. Finally he decided to get help by talking to a counselor. He learned to like himself better and to share his feelings more. He was happiest when he was with his son, Matthew. He told friends, "Everything I do is for my son."

By 1998, Mac was feeling good about himself. That was bad news for pitchers! He blasted a grand slam on Opening Day, and he never let up. On May 25, he hit his 25th homer of the season.

No one had ever hit that many home runs before June. Baseball fans were excited. They knew that Mac had a good chance to break Roger Maris's record of 61 home runs in one season.

That same day, Sammy hit two home runs, but hardly anyone noticed. Sammy still had only 11 for the season. He was nowhere near Big Mac.

But Sammy was just warming up. Suddenly, nobody could stop him. He slammed 21 homers in 22 games!

By the end of June, Mac had 37 home runs, and Sammy was right behind him with 33. The race to break the record was on!

Chapter 10

Friends and Heroes

Agence France Presse/CORBIS-Bettmann

Mark McGwire talks with Sammy Sosa at first base during a game.

All summer long, Mark McGwire and Sammy Sosa kept up their great race. People smiled when they saw how Mac and Sammy cheered for each other. Sammy kept saying, "Mark is 'The Man.' " Mark said, "Wouldn't it be great if we ended up in a tie? That would be beautiful."

On September 7, Sammy's Chicago Cubs played Mac's Cardinals in St. Louis. Sammy had 58 homers. Mac had 60 homers.

Agence France Presse/CORBIS-Bettmann

Sammy Sosa has just hit his 56th home run during the 1998 season.

Reporters asked Sammy, “Who is ‘The Man’ now?” Sammy grinned and said, “Mark is ‘The Man’ in the United States. I’m ‘The Man’ in the Dominican Republic.” Mac laughed and clapped his hands.

The St. Louis fans stood up and cheered for both Mac and Sammy. Then there was a hush as Mac came to bat in the first inning. The big man was ready. He crushed Mike Morgan’s third pitch for his 61st home run. He had tied Roger Maris!

The stadium exploded in cheers. Out in right field, Sammy Sosa was smiling and clapping. Maybe the most excited fan was Mac's father. Mac's 61st homer came on his father's 61st birthday!

Mac broke Roger Maris's record the next day. Mac was so excited that he missed first base. He had to run back and step on it.

At home plate, Mac picked up his son, Matthew, and lifted him high in the air. Sammy came running in from right field and gave Mac a big hug.

CORBIS/AFP

Sammy Sosa and Mark McGwire give each other a hug.

Then Mac ran over to the stands. He climbed up into the seats and hugged Roger Maris's grown-up children. He told them that Roger was in his heart.

Mac had broken the record, but the season wasn't over yet. Sammy told him, "Don't get too far ahead. Wait for me."

The next Sunday, Sammy tied Mac with his 62nd home run. In the stands, men and women were crying. Many were waving Dominican flags. In the Dominican Republic, people poured out into the streets to celebrate.

The amazing race went right down to the last weekend of the baseball season. On Friday, Sammy pulled ahead of Mac with his 66th home run. But that was his last homer of 1998.

45 minutes later, Big Mac hit his 66th homer. Then, in his last two games, he went out and hit four more homers! The fans shook their heads in amazement. Who could imagine 70 home runs in one season? "I can't believe I did it," Mac said afterwards. "Can you believe it?"

Agence France Presse/CORBIS-Bettmann

Mark McGwire of the St. Louis Cardinals hits his 62nd home run on September 8, 1998.

The great race was over. Both Mac and Sammy had broken a record that had lasted for 37 years. Better yet, they showed how players could compete against each other and still be friends.

Mac and Sammy also showed how to care for other people. Big Mac has given a million dollars to help children who have been hurt by adults. Sammy often sends money to help poor people back home. People in the Dominican Republic call him "Sammy Claus."

Maybe Mac and Sammy care about other people because they both have been through some hard times. Both men had to learn how to be happy. And for one magical season, they made millions of other people happy right along with them.

The End

About the Start-to-Finish® Writer

John Bergez has worked as an editor and writer since 1976. In addition to writing several Start-to-Finish titles, John has written materials for school programs in social studies, astronomy, and other subjects. As a member of the school volunteer program in Pacifica, California, he uses Start-to-Finish books in working with fourth- and fifth-grade students on reading and writing. In recognition of his volunteer work, John received the San Mateo County Reading Association's Celebrate Literacy Award for 2001.

About the Reader

Bernard Mixon is a professional actor who performs on the stage, in films, and in many television shows and commercials. On stage, Bernard has played the role of Julius Caesar at the Black Ensemble Theatre and the role of the lion in the popular play, *The Wiz.* You may have seen Bernard as Magic Sam in the television series, *America's Most Wanted,* or as Ross Thomas in *The Mary Thomas Story.*

For the past ten years, Bernard has been singing jazz, pop, country and gospel music with a band called *The Moods.* When he performs with this group, he also plays the harmonica, drums and other kinds of percussion instruments.

A Note from the Start-to-Finish® Editors

This book has been divided into approximately equal short chapters so that the student can read a chapter and take the cloze test in one reading session. This length constraint has sometimes required the authors and editors to make transitions in mid-chapter or to break up chapters in unexpected places.

You will also notice that Start-to-Finish Books look different from other high-low readers and chapter books. The text layout of this book coordinates with the other media components (CD and audiocassette) of the Start-to-Finish series.

The text in the book matches, line for line and page for page, the text shown on the computer screen, enabling readers to follow along easily in the book. Each page ends in a complete sentence so that the student can either practice the page (repeat reading) or turn the page to continue with the story. If the next sentence cannot fit on the page in its entirety, it has been shifted to the next page. For this reason, the sentence at the top of a page may not be indented, signaling that it is part of the paragraph from the preceding page.

Words are not hyphenated at the ends of lines. This sometimes creates extra space at the end of a line, but eliminates confusion for the struggling reader.